# THE MAGIC
# HAND OF
# CHANCE

# THE MAGIC HAND OF CHANCE

A *Tales of Everyday Magic* Novel

## SOPHIA MAX

### and Lynn Lauber

Based on a screenplay by Ethan Lipton

**VISIONS**

## HAY HOUSE, INC.

Carlsbad, California • New York City
London • Sydney • Johannesburg
Vancouver • Hong Kong • New Delhi

*Published* and *distributed in the United States by:* Hay House,
Inc.: www.hayhouse.com® • *Published and distributed in Australia by:* Hay House Australia Pty. Ltd.: www.hayhouse.com.au •
*Published and distributed in the United Kingdom by:* Hay House
UK, Ltd.: www.hayhouse.co.uk • *Published and distributed in
the Republic of South Africa by:* Hay House SA (Pty), Ltd.: www
.hayhouse.co.za • *Distributed in Canada by:* Raincoast: www
.raincoast.com • *Published in India by:* Hay House Publishers
India: www.hayhouse.co.in

*Cover design:* Mario San Miguel • *Interior design:* Tricia Breidenthal

**Library of Congress Control Number:** 2012938777

**Tradepaper ISBN:** 978-1-4019-3787-4
**Digital ISBN:** 978-1-4019-3788-1

Printed in the United States of America

*"My brain is the key
that sets me free."*

— HARRY HOUDINI

# PROLOGUE

I walked up the stairs to the Victorian mansion known as the Magic Castle and stopped for a moment to catch my breath. Was I really here, at this holy place? Was I really in California, surrounded by palm trees and red tropical plants that looked like flames? I closed my eyes, then opened them again, quickly. The sky looked even bluer, and the mansion even more huge and impressive. Yes, I was really here.

The giant carved doors were so thick and heavy that I couldn't open them by myself. I put my shoulder to the door and pushed; I turned the knob left, then right. I still couldn't do it. After all this time, what if I wasn't able to get inside? But I shouldn't have worried; an elegant man in a tuxedo eventually appeared.

"Good afternoon, young man," he said. "I presume you don't know about the owl."

I shook my head no. I didn't know what he was talking about.

"Well, look up to your right."

A stuffed owl sat on a perch, staring down at me.

"Tell him the password, and you'll be able to enter."

"But I don't know a password," I said, beginning to sweat. We had heard that America was very different—maybe this was what you had to do whenever you visited a new place.

"Well, what would you normally say if you wanted to enter a building?"

I thought for a moment. My English was pretty good, but not the best. "Open?"

"That's close enough. The password is 'open sesame.'"

"Open sesame," I said proudly, and the door immediately swung open. We moved into a main lobby so fancy that it took my breath away.

"Oh!" I said, in spite of myself, and then blushed.

Mirrors, golden chandeliers, a roaring fire in a fireplace. My heart thumped with excitement; there was so much to see. The man bowed and moved off to greet another visitor, dashing my hopes that he might show me around.

Although I'd heard of this castle all my life, now that I was here, I didn't know where to turn. All I knew was that there was one thing I wanted to see more than any other. I looked at the grandfather clock in the hallway; I didn't have much time.

I turned to the right and saw a small wax museum lined with figures of famous magicians. I didn't recognize the mustachioed one standing at the entrance in a velvet jacket. But I couldn't help reaching out and gingerly touching his hand, he looked so real. Next door was a library filled with more leather-bound books on magic than anyone could ever read in a lifetime. Farther down the hall was a séance room, where a table was set up for people to communicate with the dead. I peeked into each room, but I didn't hesitate for long. The thick carpet muffled the sound of my footsteps as I trudged onward until I saw the winding staircase I'd been looking for.

I gripped the railing and started making my way up. Lining the wall were portraits of the world's most famous magicians, and I recognized many of them from stories my mother had told me at bedtime. There was Howard Thurston, the King of Cards, who once ran the world's largest traveling illusion show; there was American magician Harry Blackstone, with his dark mustache, famous for my favorite trick—sawing a woman in half. There was the master of them all—Harry Houdini. And then there was a portrait of the man I knew best—a tall gentleman with slick black hair and slender fingers, who stood holding a mask of his own face. I'd seen copies of this photograph all my life, but I never got tired of staring at it. This was the magician who had changed my life.

# CHAPTER 1

In Moscow, on the eve of the Soviet Union's collapse, performing for a circus was considered a most prestigious job.

The Moscow circus was the most respected and beloved in a country that took its circuses seriously, where it was regarded as much of an art form as opera or ballet. Performers in the troupe were trained in acrobatics, clowning, juggling, and contortion at state-run training facilities.

The circus at that time was an outlet for Soviet propaganda, with many of the older acts telling stories, proverbs, or folk legends designed to advance the Soviet cause. But some performers had grown weary of state control and yearned for freedom to seek better-paid work in foreign countries. Among these performers, it wasn't uncommon to hear talk of defection. No one could quite believe that the last days of the empire were at hand or that their lives might suddenly change and become freer.

Except for Yevgeni Voronin, that is. Voronin considered himself on the way to becoming one of the great magicians of the world. Besides being a true showman, he was the dreamer of the troupe, with a soft spot for spectacle and glitz—most of which he'd read about in books or seen in movies.

The problem was that this great self had yet to emerge. But Voronin saw outlines of him in the mirror, even sitting in his dressing room, applying stage makeup for the night's performance. Voronin knew his talent would soon reveal itself to everyone; he simply had to continue rehearsing and believing in himself, and he knew it would happen.

No one would have called him handsome—but Voronin liked to think of himself as elegant, princely even, especially in certain light. At 39, he pomaded his raven black hair and applied pale makeup to his aquiline nose and lipstick to his thin lips. At six foot two inches, he was one of the tallest of the performers, and the slenderest. But he usually wore so many coats to protect himself from the bitter cold that few people even noticed.

At the rear of the auditorium that was their base when they were home, the troupe went through various motions of preparation and rehearsal. They had just returned from a monthlong tour across the Soviet Union and were soon to appear in front of a hometown crowd.

A muscle man juggled bottles as a curvy brunette walked about with a flaming torch that she would soon insert down her throat. Two golden-haired young women linked hands and practiced backflips; a clown stood smoking in the corner, a painted smile superimposed on his down-turned mouth. A young couple in sequined outfits performed handstands. There was something automatic and weary in their movements. Outside the window, a heavy snow fell like a pure white curtain.

✧　✧

Voronin got up and peeked out at the audience; given the freezing, snowy weather, the turnout was small. Only the orchestra seats were completely full, and a few of the older men looked as if they'd wandered inside to get warm and maybe sleep for a while.

"Small, eh?" Oleg, the oldest of the troupe's two clowns, asked, cigarette smoke wreathing his round, toadlike face.

"An artist doesn't perform for the crowd, but for himself," Voronin said.

"Yes, yes, this is true." Oleg smiled and gave Voronin a pat on the back as he watched him head out.

Voronin moved onto the stage and gave a formal bow before he began performing his tricks with great ceremony and care.

*Everyone deserves the best performance we can give,* he thought, smiling. *And imagine—a king or queen could be in the audience!*

He knew that some of the troupe—especially the clowns—laughed at his formal manner, but he didn't care. Magic was not just his vocation but his passion; his act may not have fully matured yet, but it would. Of this he had no doubt.

He started with a card trick, awkwardly pulling cards from the air, then, sensing the audience's disinterest, quickly proceeded to his hat trick. As he attempted to pull the red rope out from inside the hat, he ended up knocking over the entire table. He recovered and moved on with gravity and style. There were a few titters in the audience, but it was unclear whether they were laughing at his ineptitude or simply engaged in their own conversations.

Waiting to go on, the sequined young acrobatic couple watched him gravely. Voronin finally bowed as he finished his act, walked off briskly, and retreated to his dressing room. He looked at himself in the mirror. He had heard their halfhearted applause; but he would not be discouraged.

He closed his eyes for a moment, then looked up at a painting that hung on the wall no matter where he went—it was a small print of Jean-François Millet's *The Gleaners*. In the picture, a warm, golden light suffused a scene of struggle and survival—poor women removing grain from the fields after a harvest. The fatigue in the backs of the peasants never failed to move him. This had been his parents' lot in life on a farm in a western province, but it would not be his.

After he removed his stage makeup, Voronin didn't wait for the finale but decided to head straight home. He began to put on nearly all the clothing he owned: three layers of coats, two pairs of gloves, and four scarves. He was so bulked up that he could barely move his arms. He pushed hard at the stage door against the winter wind and was greeted by a great gust of frigid air and snow that nearly toppled him over.

He stood on a quiet, mostly deserted street surrounded by apartment complexes—gray blocks of stacked cement. In the treeless distance, a smoke-stack emitted a long plume of smoke.

Voronin tucked his head down and walked against the wind. There were few cars, but buses and cabs veered past, lit up in the twilight and full of black-hatted men and scarved women. After several blocks, he entered an apartment building and walked into the crumbling lobby. Mail was piled up on a table, and he was sorting through it when a door opened and a middle-aged woman holding a large yellow cat stuck out her head.

"Hello, Mrs. Komarov. How's the neuritis?"

The woman stomped out using a cane, letting the cat down to rub against Voronin.

"Worse than ever—the cold weather, you know. Leopold knows your walk. He wanted to see you."

Voronin picked up several envelopes from the mail pile, then bent down to rub the cat's head.

"You need a pet yourself," Mrs. Komarov said, looking down at him. "It's no good for a man to live alone."

"Ah, you're probably right, but I travel so much," Voronin stood and looked toward Mrs. Komarov's apartment. "Should I come in and visit Ivan?"

Mrs. Komarov said, "Do you have time? Just one little trick—it cheers him so."

Voronin went inside, where a teenage boy sat in a chair at the table; by the twist of his back and the way he canted to one side, it was clear that he was crippled.

"Hello, Mr. Voronin."

"Hello, Ivan. It's cold out today, eh? I thought I'd just come in for a small bowl of soup." He looked at Mrs. Komarov, who went into the kitchen and brought out a bowl and a spoon.

He sat down across from Ivan and took the spoon; before dipping it into the soup, he said, "My, this spoon looks crooked, let me see if I can straighten it." He pressed down, making the spoon appear as if it were bending in half.

The boy laughed out loud. "Look at that, Mother. He ruined your good spoon!"

"So sorry. Maybe another."

Mrs. Komarov bustled in and out of the kitchen, bringing one piece of flatware after another. He "bent" another spoon, then a fork and knife, a gravy ladle, and two butter knives. He had some trouble with the knives, but Ivan didn't seem to notice. As Voronin rose to go, he noticed that Ivan's face had softened and there was a rose tint in his pale cheeks.

"Thanks, Voronin," Mrs. Komarov said at the door. "You always do him good."

Taking his mail, Voronin climbed three flights of stairs, then opened the door to enter the tiny corner apartment where he'd lived for more than 20 years. The plaster walls were cracked, and a wind flapped at the threadbare blinds that had been pulled down over the windows. The only items visible in the half light were a small cot, neatly made up, a vanity table, with props piled on it, and a kitchen table with two chairs. Voronin tried to flip on an overhead light, but it flickered and went out, so he walked over and raised the blinds. He removed his scarves, coats, and gloves and threw them on a coatrack, then put a kettle on the stove and lit the flame. After making a cup of tea, he sat down and opened the mail.

After opening several envelopes, he found an official-looking one, and his eyes lit up. He read the letter aloud: "The Ministry of Culture requests a meeting with you. Please appear at the Ministry building at 9:00 A.M., Wednesday morning."

Voronin bolted from his chair, knocking it over. "The Ministry of Culture requests a meeting! This must be good news!"

He paced around the apartment, then opened the door and looked out into the hallway, hoping there was someone he could share the news with. He opened the window and let in a gust of snowy wind but shut it quickly. He realized the only people he really wanted to talk to were the troupe, and he'd see them in the morning anyway—at work.

He quickly changed out of his work clothes, then put his coats back on. Then he lay down on his bed and held the letter to his chest.

"This must be good news!" he said out loud again, and within minutes, he was fast asleep.

◇  ◇

In the morning, Voronin gulped down a cup of tea and ate a piece of buttered bread. Then he threw on his clothes and peered into a mirror to comb his hair. He dressed again in the extra coats before clattering down the stairs and walking back out into the snow, moving more rapidly than before. Ahead of him was the ornate but decrepit building that housed the Ministry of Culture. Entering the freezing lobby, he found that the rest of the circus troupe was also lined up against the wall.

"Ah, you all were also invited?" he asked as he approached.

Dmitri called out, "Oh, you thought the boss just wanted to speak to you?"

Voronin shrugged as he sat down at the end of the line. He would have never admitted to it, but that was exactly what he'd hoped, that this message was going to be some commendation or honor especially for him.

They'd crisscrossed the country together in a convoy of buses and freezing trains—to Vyborg, with its ancient castles; Sochi, on the Black Sea; and remote Tomsk, with its relics of wooden architecture. The troupe members were proud to be part of a tradition that had started centuries before, during the time of Catherine the Great, when the circus was a highly popular entertainment form that appealed to all of Russian society, regardless of social class, education, or age.

But to the troupe, these tours had grown tedious. They had already seen the lakes and mountains and monuments. These did not make up for the cold showers, endless lines, and bland food on the road. Everyone pined for new horizons, and no one more than Voronin, who envisioned travel as a component of the new, rich life he was sure he'd enjoy one day as a famous magician.

His chronic optimism rubbed off on the others, who automatically counted on him to keep up their spirits. But he softened at the sight of the troupe's weary profiles. They had been together for so long that they'd become a large extended family with their own roles and alliances.

They all looked so glum that he began to wander down the aisle, to see if he might cheer them up, bypassing Dmitri and Oleg, who were locked in a private argument.

The troupe was growing restive—smoking cigarettes, muttering complaints. Some of them had begun to stretch or rehearse their acts. A young blonde woman did a double cartwheel that brought her up flush with Voronin.

"Oh, excuse me, Voronin! I didn't see you there."

"Nice form, Katia," he said, as she gave him a pert bow, then sat back down with her sisters, Katerina and Klara, who both were seated, holding hefty textbooks in their laps.

The acrobatic Ovinkos served as the troupe's virginal daughters, though by now, in their late 20s, their exact status was no longer clear. They were three variations on a single theme—brainy, with long, slender necks and wide eyes. Two were blondes, and the eldest was a brunette.

"This cuts into our study time," Katerina, the eldest, complained to Voronin.

Klara agreed. "With work and rehearsals, we only have two hours a day."

"Your father would be very proud of your dedication," Voronin said gravely.

Viktor, their father, had been a friend of Voronin's, an acrobat in the troupe who had assured his daughters that they could pursue their educations once he retired. But not long after, he'd died of an unexpected heart attack, so they made a pact to begin their studies at once. It had been six years since Viktor's death, and they still toted around their textbooks wherever they went. At night, when they finished rehearsals and performances, they read together in the same bed under heavy wool blankets. All three dreamed of entering the medical field one day: their textbooks included medical immunology, human physiology, and *Gray's Anatomy.*

Sitting next to them were Xavier and Zoe, glamorous trapeze artists and the only married couple in the troupe; such was their happiness that even after 20 years of marital bliss, they kept entirely to themselves. They only had eyes for each other.

Beside them, Irena and Lev sat together, rolling wooden dowels under their feet to limber them up. Irena and Lev were partners in a handstand act and had been together for many years—since they were teenagers. Irena was still as fresh and lovely as a fairy-tale princess, with her cascading blonde hair and ethereal face. Lev, with his blond curls and athletic physique, was equally handsome, but for some reason, the two remained unmarried.

"So how are the lovebirds?" Voronin asked.

"Good, Voronin," Irena said with a half smile, but Lev made a snorting sound.

"We're tired, like everyone. If he sends us on tour again, I think I will defect."

"You will not," Irena insisted.

"I will!" Lev flared. "I'm still young and able— why should they always tie me down?"

"But your sweet lady here," Voronin said. "Surely you would never leave her?"

Lev eyed Irena and shrugged. "Of course, she can also come."

Irena rolled her eyes at Svetlana, who was in the midst of practicing a front bend. It was rare to find Svetlana in any normal human position; she seemed always to be splitting, folding, or twisting her body into an elaborate pretzel of flesh.

15

Svetlana was ten years Irena's senior, and the young woman's adviser and confidante. She had been born into the circus and had always assumed that she'd get out in time to pursue other careers or get married, but somehow it had never happened. She'd become caught up in the traveling camaraderie and deeply ingrained habits of circus life. It was useless to catch the eye of a handsome, eligible man on these trips because she was gone by the next week, packed up with the troupe and off to another town. Her attachments were to the people she traveled and worked with, with whom she had created a strong, unbreakable bond.

Some nights as she sat in her room, knitting a long black scarf meant for no one, she wondered whether she would ever find love.

Voronin couldn't help noticing how the color of her soft, brown hair complemented the peach tint of her skin. Normally, he saw Svetlana in her costume—a pink wig and heavy makeup, both of which made her resemble a ragdoll that had been tossed about.

"I don't know how you do this," he marveled aloud as she unwound and stood up.

"Well, Voronin, I do not know how you do your tricks, either!"

He felt himself blushing; he wasn't used to compliments, especially from ladies. He knew he wasn't as good as he wanted to be, as he *would be* one day with continued work and dedication. Yet even when his tricks were marred by miscues or mistakes, the troupe tolerated the flaws in his performance, just as they did his endless schemes for a glorious future.

"A little practice, a little patience," he said to Svetlana. "It's all in the mind—success and failure. You have to believe in yourself!"

A waft of smoke made Voronin cough and Svetlana turn her head. It was Svetlana's roommate, Mariska, dressed in one of her tight, form-fitting dresses, dramatically inhaling a cigarette.

"You aren't supposed to smoke in here," Svetlana said in irritation.

"I'm a fire eater. What do you expect?" Mariska said in her world-weary accent. "I'm just rehearsing like you. Inhaling fire—it is all the same concept."

"I thought you gave up cigarettes and vodka," Voronin said.

"Oh, did you? Since when were you so interested in my personal habits, Voronin?"

Voronin turned away without answering; Mariska's sarcastic tone made him nervous; he never knew what to say when she turned her bitter tongue on him.

The rest of the troupe was locked in conversation; a quartet of male buddies was talking in a confidential circle: Peter Pitofsky, the ringmaster, flamboyant and campy, with his spiked golden hair and heavy makeup; Sergey, the handsome playboy juggler; Rustam, the aerialist, a serious introvert; and Matvei, who served both as clown and emcee.

Voronin headed back to his seat, where Dmitri and Oleg were in the final stage of their heated discussion.

These two were the troupe's jokey uncles, and they had been in the circus since they were boys. They were the quintessential odd couple. Dmitri was tall, dark, and handsome; Oleg, stout and stocky. But under their makeup, they looked far from funny, with bags under their eyes and a chronic slump in their shoulders. Voronin sat down in the chair where he'd left his top hat and tuned in to their conversation:

"So, maybe you'll get sent to Siberia," Oleg said.

"Siberia? For taking one can of chocolate sauce?"

Oleg shrugged. "I'm tired of talking about it."

But Dmitri wasn't. "You're crazy," he said with a snort. "Siberia? No." He thought for a moment. "Mongolia, maybe, but not Siberia."

Voronin asked, "Do you think they will send us back on tour?"

Oleg laughed bitterly. "Oh, sure: Siberia to Mongolia and back again."

Voronin said, "Well, not me. I'm going to America!"

Oleg elbowed him, and Dmitri shushed him, saying loud enough for everyone to hear, "America again! Ha-ha, nice joke." Then he whispered, "You know you can't say that here—"

"I don't even want to go to America," Oleg said. "Growing up, all I heard was that America was going to strike our homeland at any time."

But Voronin ignored him; he leaned closer and said in a hushed voice, "I'm going to the Magic Castle in California—the most prestigious magician's society in the world. This, for a magician, is the most beautiful place. One day, my picture will be on the wall next to Houdini's."

This dream was an old one for Voronin; he'd developed it years ago in order to survive as the bullied son of his village's poorest family. Back then, he was taunted for the holes in his shoes and for his gaunt face, which looked old and world-weary far before its time.

It was a face not unlike those on the statues of the gold-domed Russian orthodox church, where his mother had herded the family each Sunday morning. He and his four sisters sat in a motley row amidst the gilt and incense and ornate language, and Voronin, at least for an hour or two, felt safe and warm.

The other children also made fun of his parents —his father, who spent half the day picking through the neighbors' garbage, foraging for enough to feed his family, and the rest of the time drinking in order to forget what he'd done, while his mother, with her wizened, apple cheeks and red bandana, bent over the fields of wheat.

Voronin viewed all this as a boy and made a conscious decision to concentrate elsewhere, on some point higher and brighter. One of his uncles was an old-time performer who used to teach him tricks whenever he visited. He pulled scarves out of his shirtsleeves and cards from under his cap. Voronin studied his uncle's every move because he'd discovered that people paid attention to him whenever he performed one of those acts of magic, even when he bungled it, even when it was as simple as making a coin disappear in his palm.

"How'd you do that?" the boys who had previously taunted Voronin asked.

And not just the boys, but the girls, the same ones who had never given him the time of day before, who wore their hair in complicated braids that he pondered as they sat in class, braids the color of oak and thick as rope. There was something almost helpless in the way they watched him, when he stood on the corner and spun his magic.

"Oh, Voronin!" they cried in new, respectful voices, when he "guessed" the card they picked. "That is amazing!"

Even when he started working the wheat fields himself, he continued to practice magic. He saw that people yearned to believe in magic in one form or another. It made them feel as if some other force was in the world, one that they could not see or control, that might one day benefit them as well.

Houdini was Voronin's hero, and Voronin took pleasure in the fact that there were many similarities in their lives. Houdini had been born in Budapest, another cold, hard place. He was brought to America by his rabbi father and was so poor that he had to work as a bootblack. That is, until his father took him to see a traveling magician and his interest in performance took over.

Houdini was self-confident and had a flair for exaggeration; he knew how to keep audiences interested—these were traits Voronin craved to possess.

Voronin knew even as a boy that he would have to leave the Soviet Union in order to become a real success, so he traveled on buses to dusty libraries, then sat for hours over books studying photographic plates of exotic places. *Figure 2. The canals of Amsterdam. Figure 6: The Louvre, bathed in golden light.* It didn't matter that these books were ancient. These cities and their splendors would live on; they would wait for him whenever he eventually, inevitably arrived. He would follow in Houdini's tracks and jump into the Seine in Paris, escape from handcuffs at Scotland Yard, be locked upside down in a Chinese torture cell.

Whenever he got discouraged, he reminded himself that for many years, Houdini's career went nowhere.

But it was the sunny prosperity of America, specifically California, that most captured Voronin's imagination. This was his dream destination, the one that surpassed all others.

Voronin searched the libraries until he found a color photo that epitomized an American world so perfect that it nearly made him swoon. A smiling family cruised down a flawless highway in a red convertible—the Hollywood sign looming in the background. The wind was in their hair, lifting the curls of the mother and daughter just so, but not ruffling the palm trees or disturbing the dark, manly locks of father and son. The sun hung low in the endless blue sky.

For all his life, this would be his favorite photo; he went into the lavatory and carefully cut it out with his pocket knife, his first and only crime. This could be, *would* be, him someday.

Later, Voronin discovered the most important fact of all—that Houdini's photo and a replica of his séance room were in Los Angeles's Magic Castle, a magnificent Victorian mansion that was a showplace for the greatest magicians from around the world. He had read about this Shangri-la in a forbidden newspaper that had been smuggled in by the son of a cousin who had defected.

He read how the Magic Castle was a private clubhouse and home for the Academy of Magical Arts, a special organization devoted to the advancement of the ancient art. The purpose of the academy was to encourage and promote public interest in magic, with particular emphasis on preserving its history as an art form, entertainment, and hobby. Beginning with a charter membership of 150, the academy had grown into a world-renowned fraternal organization with a membership of nearly 5,000.

*Soon to be 5,001,* Voronin thought.

# CHAPTER 2

Voronin emerged from his reverie, opened his eyes, and shook himself alert. He had to pay attention to where he was: sitting in a hardbacked chair in the Ministry of Culture. Dmitri and Oleg were still beside him, arguing away. He looked at his watch; they had been waiting for nearly 50 minutes to hear whatever the minister had to say.

Just then, the door to the office finally opened, and they all roused themselves and stood like soldiers, their posture as straight as could be.

"Finally," Oleg said under his breath as they began filing in.

Usually when the minister met with them, there was bad news on the horizon. Someone had been caught breaking a rule, or there was a warning about decorum, dress, or drunken behavior. The minister, a former military man who still dressed in full regalia, loved nothing more than to chastise them for infractions; there were so many things they could do wrong.

His office was even darker and colder than the lobby, and it featured ancient wooden desks and messy piles of paper covered with official stamps and seals. Standing shoulder to shoulder in two tight rows, the troupe assembled, various looks of hope and exhaustion etched across their faces.

The minister was a hard little man with an elaborate comb-over and tiny glasses that accentuated his bloodshot eyes. He was rigidly militaristic and liked to keep the troupe tethered by an endless litany of regulations that encompassed nearly everything that they naturally wanted to do. These rules seemed designed with one goal in mind: to minimize all pleasure.

Today he addressed them with his common tone of pomp and arrogance. Once they'd all filed in and stood at attention against the wall, he announced, "Today I have positive news. You have been selected to embark upon an extensive international tour."

The troupe gasped with surprise and turned to smile at one another, thrilled by the news. Voronin grabbed Dmitri's hand in his excitement, but Dmitri quickly pulled it away. The minister, however, scowled at their faces and with his next words cut off their expressions of pleasure.

"You're smiling? You think this will be a vacation? You think you are going on holiday? Please be advised: you are going to work—for your country. You will be traveling through many hostile territories across the continent.

"Your accommodations will be spartan. Your pay will be small, and we advise you to save what little you make. You will be supervised at all times, and your presence will be confined to the circus grounds, the hotel, and anywhere else Comrade Konstantin Vasilyev says you shall go."

Konstantin, a tall, grim man with brown hair and narrow eyes, moved out of the background and made a slight, formal nod, then retreated again.

"And if there ever is confusion as to where that might be, Comrade Vladimir Demidov will explain it to you."

Vladimir stood; he looked like a bodyguard with his receding hair, serious expression, and intimidating size.

"Never forget that the Soviet Union is the only country with a university devoted to the circus arts and has been since 1919! Remember that only here do performers receive such serious training in gymnastics to utilize within the circus arena.

"Remember your legacy and uphold it! Since the Moscow circus began touring, we have provided an impressive selection of performances, which have influenced contemporary circuses across the world. These performances promote our values! This is where you're from—this is the reputation you are expected to uphold."

They had heard this speech many times. Dmitri stood at the front with his eyes crossed, and Oleg fought back a guffaw. But Voronin always found this speech so stirring that it almost made him cry, never mind that he was desperate to leave the country. He was still moved by this history that he was part of, no matter where he ended up in the future.

The minister continued, "So here are the rules. Do not wander off for a midnight stroll. Do not consort with foreigners, in particular, Spaniards and Danes. There will be no carousing. Shenanigans will not be tolerated. And under no circumstance will you engage in monkey business! You may have a small celebration in the event of birthdays or good news, as is the tradition, but that's it! Your purpose is to entertain and bring glory to your country. Please do so with great care."

With stiff military carriage, the minister exited. There was an extended moment of silence after his exit, then the performers exploded in a cheer.

◇　◇

The next morning, bulked up again in all his coats, a suitcase in one hand, his top hat in the other, Voronin surveyed his apartment. The blinds had been pulled down and the lights turned off. It sat neat and bleak, as if no one had ever lived there. It had been assigned to him so many years ago now that he could barely remember living anywhere else. He was surprised to realize that he had a lump in his throat, as if he were leaving behind a boring but steadfast friend.

He shut his door with great solemnity, as if trying not to wake up whomever might be left behind. He began to walk down the hall, then turned around and returned to the apartment. Inside, he peeled off three of his top coats and hung them on the coatrack. Then, wearing only a black, fitted wool coat, he left the apartment again.

When he reached the downstairs, he stood in front of Ivan's door and hesitated, unsure of what to do. While he was deciding, the door cracked open and Mrs. Komarov looked out silently, first at his face, then at his suitcase.

"You are going away?" she whispered.

He nodded. "Yes—far away."

"Will you be back this time?"

He hesitated. "I hope not."

She nodded.

"What do you think I should do about Ivan?"

She thought for a moment.

"Maybe we let him sleep. Saying good-bye to you—I think this would be too sad for him today. I won't even mention it, unless he does."

Voronin still hesitated.

"Don't feel bad," Ivan's mother said. "You made him very happy over the years. He believes in magic now. Just remember us, that's all."

Voronin's eyes were damp. "How could I forget?" he asked. He gave her a brief hug, then turned back as he headed out the front door, and into the snowy morning. "Tell Ivan I will see him again. I promise."

✧ ✧

Twenty minutes later, Voronin climbed into a large bus with the rest of the troupe and took a window seat, placing his top hat in his lap. It was early morning, but everyone had a shiny, hushed look of excitement on their faces. They were finally escaping, however briefly. Behind them a convoy of two other buses full of the sets, costumes, and complex equipment required to put on a show were also warming up. They were conspicuous by the red and blue script on the sides of the buses—*Moscow Traveling Circus*—along with the brightly colored paintings of a sequined lady, a bullnecked muscleman, and a black-haired magician far younger and more handsome than Voronin, with his sexy blonde assistant.

As the engines revved up, the buses shuddered to a start and began moving slowly through the streets. Voronin pressed his face against the window and watched the bleak landscape, with its bare trees and tall, featureless buildings. Skinny dogs with their ribs showing barked as they passed by. Reflected in the glass, Voronin's face showed a combination of longing, fear, and wonder. After miles of apartments, statues, and factories, there were suddenly patches of field and meadow, then small villages. In one, an elderly woman in a black scarf leaned on a broom in a doorway and raised her arm to wave.

Voronin was the only one who waved back. "Good-bye," he whispered. "Good-bye, old country."

# CHAPTER 3

It took over 30 hours to travel from Moscow to a small town outside of Zurich. Most of the troupe slept during the trip, but Voronin kept a little notebook and filled pages with his impressions and thoughts about Belarus, Poland, and Germany, as they passed through them.

"We have traveled nearly two thousand seven hundred kilometers, or one thousand six hundred seventy-seven miles!" he announced proudly when the bus finally creaked to a halt and the troupe blearily stumbled out.

They had stopped along the way to use the facilities at different stations, but it was only now, in the cool, high air, that they all could appreciate the beauty of the alpine landscape.

"One hour!" Konstantin announced when the troupe harangued him for just a little time to look around. Since they had never traveled beyond the borders of the Soviet Union, they were drawn to the first gift shops they encountered and arrived back at the hotel with the most clichéd souvenirs. They bought Swiss national flags and blocks of cheese and chocolates in gold foil wrapping. Oleg and Dmitri both bought alpine hats with green feathers in the bands; Sergey practiced his yodeling.

Voronin, the last in, came back with nothing but a map and an expression of utter delight on his face. "I took a tram and saw the Alps, steel architecture, and many banks. There is so much money here! Also, I ate cheese fondue."

His face was flushed with excitement. Konstantin and Vladimir exchanged bemused looks.

"Okay, you've had your fun. It's time to work now," Konstantin said.

As they filed by, the concierge smiled widely from his post behind the front desk, greeting each troupe member: "*Wilkommen. Wilkommen.*"

Many cities had grand theaters and halls that the troupe could perform in, but the circus always performed in a canvas big top whenever they traveled; it was erected by the workmen who followed in specially equipped buses. This tent was occasionally set up on a vacant lot or in a field, as it was today.

Valentine, the troupe's handyman, supervised the workmen and also worked discreetly in the wings overseeing the technical staff. "Carpenters, at your posts. Hey, you—be careful with the lights!"

Nails were hammered into wood. The vast canvas tent was pulled up with cables and ropes, then tied to stakes. Red and white and 125 feet round, the European-style big top had been built in France and seated as many as 1,500 people. Once it was up, the tent interior was decorated with ornate touches: a red carpet was rolled onto the floor, a chandelier hoisted, a theater curtain hung. This procedure took several hours to complete.

Konstantin watched as Valentine finally opened the curtain, revealing the opulent interior. Theater lights were turned into place, shining directly into a lens; candles were lit.

Meanwhile, Voronin sat in front of the mirror in his tiny dressing room, wearing his top hat and practicing tricks with his deck of cards until Valentine came to see whether he needed anything.

Voronin pointed at his table. "My prop table needs more support so it doesn't fall. Can you fix it?"

Valentine bent down and studied it as Konstantin passed by, checking his watch. "Five more minutes, we go on."

Valentine told Voronin, "Sorry, there's no time. I'll have to fix it for you later."

As Valentine rushed off, Voronin looked at himself in the mirror for a moment, then took a deep breath.

He heard a drumroll, then Peter's voice in introduction. At the next drumroll, Peter would do a flip and the show would begin.

Dmitri and Oleg leaped onto the stage and chased Peter around the ring, honking horns, falling down, and pulling up their pants as the crowd roared in approval. Their faces were painted white, and they wore round red noses and floppy over-sized shoes. Dmitri's persona was doleful, while Oleg's was more manic. They continually tripped, did backflips, and pinched each other. Their actions looked natural, even childlike, yet both had been trained in drama and acting and had attended the clown studio at the Moscow circus.

They ran off the stage to squeals of delight and thunderous applause. "We make people laugh, we bring them joy, what other job does this?" Oleg said, panting heavily and sweating.

Matvei introduced the Ovinko sisters, who bounded onto the stage, performing acrobatics. Dressed in white lacy unitards with garters, their long hair pulled back tightly, the sisters did a series of daring somersaults through flaming hoops. Then they performed twists and turns on a rope suspended high in the air. The audience craned their necks and watched with fear, then cheered with delight as the sisters bowed and ran backstage smiling.

When Svetlana came onstage in her pink wig and heavy makeup, she performed a series of splits that seemed physically impossible. But at her finale —a puppet contortion during which her arms seemed to come off—the crowd roared out loud.

After Sergey, who juggled hats and hoops while riding on a unicycle, it would be time for Voronin. He stood in the wings, nervously waiting to go on. He was surprised by how anxious he was. He had always believed that if he were bathed in an atmosphere of freedom, all his talent would co-alesce and his act would become better than ever.

He reached into his pocket, looking for the photo of California, part of a small bag of talis-mans he carried with him wherever he went, but he couldn't find it. He cast about for something else to hold on to—Houdini, that was it. Hadn't his hero said something about fear that was use-ful? He rifled through his little notebook. He'd written it down there, he was sure.

Then he found it: "My chief task has been to conquer fear. . . . The public sees only the thrill of the accomplished trick; they have no conception of the tortuous preliminary self-training that was necessary to conquer fear. . . . No one except my-self can appreciate how I have to work at this job every single day, never letting up for a moment." Voronin read this quote twice in a row, then took a deep breath as Matvei made his introduction.

"Ladies and gentleman, next we have a magi-cian so tricky we didn't even know he was in the show until the curtain went up: Please welcome Yevgeni Petrovich Voronin!"

"Good luck," Dmitri called out as Voronin glided onstage.

He looked out into the audience as he began his signature trick, pulling a series of cards out of the air. He liked to find someone sympathetic to look at as he performed, but the lights were so dim that he could barely make out faces in the audi-ence; there was only a slight golden sheen—this was because so many blonde-haired Swiss women were in the audience, he realized.

When he made a bouquet of flowers appear from behind his back, the audience lightly applauded. He set the flowers in a vase on the prop table, which fell over, just as he'd feared it would. He picked it up, then quickly moved on to another trick. From the wings, Svetlana, Lev, and Irena watched.

Voronin set his top hat on the table and began to pull a rope from it like a snake charmer. But then the rope began to retract into the hat instead of coming out of it. He grabbed for it, reaching into the hat to pull. Meanwhile, his coat sleeve became caught on something inside the hat and when he finally pulled the rope out again, his sleeve ripped with a loud, tearing sound.

A murmur of consternation mixed with embarrassed laughter swept the audience, mingling with light applause. Unsure of what to do, Voronin stared out blankly before the troupe waved him offstage. As he approached, Irena gave Svetlana a little shove so that she was the first person he passed. She squeezed his arm as he hurried by. Lev and Irena bounced onto the stage and began their handstand act.

Back in the dressing room, Voronin examined his ripped sleeve, then sat for a moment.

He looked at himself in the mirror, then said out loud to himself, "It's okay. I must practice more. That's all. No being discouraged."

He put the hat in front of him and began again.

When all the acts were finished, there was wild applause, and Lev stuck his head around his doorway. "Voronin, come out, we're done!"

Voronin's brow was knit as he sat with the rope, pulling it in and out of the hat with great concentration. "No, no, I must practice. You go on."

Backstage, the troupe hugged each other, in high spirits as Konstantin watched with his usual stern face. The applause continued and grew even louder.

"Encore!" Peter cried.

They ran back out and received even more tremendous applause.

When they returned backstage, Konstantin was there waiting for them. He gave them a severe look. "Okay, that's enough. Well done, everyone. You have fifteen minutes to pack."

He walked off. The troupe members, deflated, dispersed to gather their things.

◇  ◇

Back at the hotel, they walked down a narrow hallway, their rooms on either side. As Konstantin and Vlad supervised, the performers lazily strolled off into their rooms, singing a Russian folk song together as they went.

When Konstantin shushed them, they continued in a quiet hum until they were all in their rooms with the doors shut. But behind the doors, there still was audible humming.

Konstantin called out for all to hear, "Does anyone have twenty-five rubles I can borrow?"

There was a sudden, utter silence.

Konstantin looked knowingly at Vladimir. "That's what I thought," he said and walked down the hall to his own room.

✧   ✧

When Svetlana left her room for the bathroom, Irena furtively followed her in.

"We have to talk. Please. I'm getting desperate about Lev. We're supposed to be engaged, but he treats me like a sister. You must give me advice. How can I get him to take me seriously?"

Svetlana studied her friend for a moment.

"You must be more forthright in letting him know how you feel. Use more endearments when you speak to him. Make your love more obvious. Maybe he does not realize how deep your emotions are."

"But of course he does! He must. Why else would I stay with him all these years and see no others?"

"You are partners . . . that doesn't mean you're in love with him anymore. Men are very dense."

Irena looked at her levelly. "Okay, I will try." She studied Svetlana. "And what about you? You're still a young woman. You also should have love in your life."

"Don't worry. For now, we will think of you."

Irena hugged her and began to leave, but Svetlana stopped her.

"Wait a minute. I have an idea. Give this to Lev." From her bag, she took out the black scarf she had been knitting for months and handed it to Irena. It was so long by now that it nearly touched the ground. "Tell him you made it for him. Men like this kind of thing. It makes you seem domestic, but not too much."

"Oh, I could never take this," Irena said. "It was so much work for you. Plus, he's never seen me knit a stitch."

"Tell him you did it at night while he slept. He won't notice anyway. I told you, men are dense and easy to fool."

Irena smiled and hugged her again. "Then why do we want them so much?"

Svetlana shrugged. "We just do."

After Svetlana left, Irena spent some extra time in the mirror, brushing her hair, and unbuttoning her nightgown so she looked more alluring. Then she walked back into their room to find Lev watching a chef prepare a cheese sauce on a Swiss cooking show.

He didn't even look up when she entered.

"What is this?" he said irritably to the television and tried to change the channel, but there was nothing else on. Irena sat next to him on the bed, in what she hoped was an appealing position.

"Lev?"

"Yes?" he asked, still staring at the TV.

"It's so nice to travel like this together, to spend some time in different places, isn't it?"

He made a vague affirmative sound and continued to watch the television.

"Lev, I have something for you."

"What is it?"

She pulled out the scarf, all five feet of it, and held it up proudly.

"What is it? A blanket?"

"No, a scarf—knit especially for you!"

"By who?"

"By me—who do you think? Try it on."

He took it and wound it around his neck so many times that it became a thick wad. He looked dubiously at her. "Well, it's warm."

"Do you like it?"

"Sure. Thanks." But he didn't seem particularly impressed by the scarf, which looked as if it were nearly strangling him.

"What would you like to do now?" she asked, shifting to another provocative pose, as he unwound the scarf.

He looked at her for a moment. "Let's talk," he said.

"Yes? I mean, yes! Yes, love, let's talk," she said, encouraged.

Lev hesitated for a moment, as if considering a serious question. "Can we be honest?"

"Yes!" Irena said, moving closer to him. "Of course. We must!"

He stopped again.

"Yes, love. Yes?"

"Am I balding?" Lev blurted out. "Back here." He turned his head. "Can you see scalp?"

Irena looked crestfallen, but she leaned forward and examined him anyway.

There was a large patch of scalp, pink and shining, at the top of his head, but she still said, "No, Lev, you're not balding at all."

"Are you sure?"

"Yes, love."

"Phew, I was starting to worry. So. Okay."

He gave her a wide smile, turned to the television again, and studied the chef.

"I wonder what this guy is making," he said.

✧ ✧

Voronin shared a room at the end of the hall with Rustam the aerialist, who lay snoring while the magician determinedly practiced his hat and rope trick, the one that had failed at the show. His top hat fell to the floor, waking Rustam, who groaned.

"Don't you ever stop working, Voronin?"

Voronin looked at him in surprise. "Of course I never stop. Did Galileo stop? Did Michelangelo stop? Did Houdini? Of course not. And it's not an option for me either."

"Okay, okay." Rustam shook his head, punched his pillow, and closed his eyes again.

✧ ✧

In Mariska and Svetlana's room, Mariska did her nails while Svetlana brushed her pink wig.

Mariska asked, "Do you have a smoke?"

"No. I quit, as you well know."

"Well, I did too, but I still enjoy one now and then." She continued with her nails, then looked at Svetlana. "Maybe Ernest will have some for me later."

"Ernest? Who's that?"

Mariska shrugged. "A new friend. A banker; he's old and very rich. I met him in the lobby. We're having dinner."

"Married?"

"Who knows?"

Mariska seemed to have no scruples, and Svetlana couldn't help but make a small face of disapproval. She and Mariska had only been placed as roommates because of the similarity of their situations—both in their late 30s, both single—though in fact they were entirely different.

Mariska had been married and divorced twice before and had a world-weary, jaded view of men, whom she saw only as sex partners or sources of money to be exploited whenever possible. With her lean beauty, long mahogany-colored hair, sculpted nails, and haughty demeanor, she often attracted portly older businessmen who bought her gold trinkets, fur-lined hats, and leather boots.

"This is all I want now," she often told Svetlana. "I'm not interested in love anymore."

"Well, you worked fast," Svetlana said, looking at her. "But we're not in our own country, and according to Konstantin, this would be considered fraternizing—"

Mariska cut her off with a laugh. "Konstantin! He would fraternize himself, if he could get away with it." She stood and shook out her hair. "There is no reason to be a nun, is there? Life—it is too short."

She moved into the bathroom. Svetlana stopped brushing for a moment and watched as her roommate shut the door.

◇　◇

In their room, Dmitri and Oleg traded a bottle of vodka back and forth as they spoke in hushed tones, the lights out.

"It's not right," Dmitri said. "We work our hearts out, we should be allowed to celebrate. We're artists, not mules! What again are the party occasions?"

Oleg sighed. "How many times have I told you? Birthdays and good news."

"Birthdays and good news," Dmitri repeated. "This is a joke."

"My father was in the symphony. It was the same for him."

"When is the next birthday?"

"Svetlana, I think. In April."

"April? Oleg, I won't make it! If I go two weeks without a party, I break out in hives."

"So what can we do?"

Dmitri said, "We must get some good news from someplace . . . or make some."

Oleg said, "Well, I don't want any."

"Why not?"

"Because whoever gets it has to pay for the party. It's tradition. I'm still trying to pay off my unicycle."

"Then somebody else must receive it."

"But who?" Oleg asked.

"We will think of someone."

# CHAPTER 4

The next morning, Voronin sat practicing his coin trick on the bus next to Sergey, who was half asleep. The coin, which was supposed to disappear into his fist, kept falling visibly into his lap, then onto the floor. He practiced over and over. All at once he looked over at Svetlana, who was knitting something new, using round needles and a bright blue color. Although she was still across the aisle, she'd moved to sit a row closer.

She glanced up and noticed him looking at her.

"Voronin, can I ask you question?" she asked.

He smiled. "Of course."

"Do you know what size hat you wear?"

He took his top hat from under the seat in front of him and punched it to its full height. He held it up so she could see. "This is the only hat I own, but I don't know the size."

"Can I see?"

He handed it to her, and she studied it from all angles, then put it on her head. She looked so comically cute that Voronin laughed out loud. Svetlana handed the hat back to him.

"So why do you ask?" Voronin asked as he took it.

"No reason," she said airily and picked up her knitting again.

He leaned back in his seat, slightly nonplussed, just as Sergey stirred. Voronin looked over at him; he felt suddenly anxious, as if he needed to talk to someone, anyone.

"Sergey, did I ever tell you that the Magic Castle is so exclusive that you have to be a magician or the friend of one in order to go?"

"Mm-hmm."

"And you need to know a secret code to make certain doors open." He couldn't help himself; he rattled on. "When it was built, it was the largest mansion in Hollywood—it's a private club, you know, where only the very best are able to join."

Sergey made another sound of assent.

"When you get there—first you catch a bus to Hollywood, but after you get to the Magic Castle, if they let you in, if they take you as one of their own, you are given a key to a secret room. And you are the only one who has the key to this room. It is your own secret room in the Magic Castle, with your own secret key."

A row ahead of him, shrunk down in their seats so only their eyes were visible, sat Oleg and

Dmitri. As they listened to Voronin's plans, Oleg nudged Dmitri, and they smirked, their eyes meeting. Here was a way to justify having a party: they could provide the unsuspecting Voronin with some much anticipated good news.

◇　◇

When the troupe checked into their hotel in Florence, they all took in their surroundings.

"Florence! Cradle of the Renaissance! The Uffizi, the Duomo!" Voronin exclaimed. "Six hundred forty-three kilometers or four hundred miles!"

After a quick stop in the hotel gift shop, Dmitri and Oleg wore black sunglasses and smoked Italian cigarettes, and Lev carried a miniature statue of David under his arm.

"No vodka here," Oleg called as they dragged their luggage inside. "*Vino!* Even for lunch. Even the babies drink it!"

"Well, there's no time for sightseeing," Konstantin insisted. "You have to work."

"But it's Florence!" Voronin said.

"You will lose your wallets or your hearts here, one or another," Konstantin said. "This is no place for peasants like you. You will stay close by—no hanky-panky!"

At the front desk, with the Italian flag hanging on the wall, the concierge greeted the troupe: "*Benvenuti. Benvenuti. Ciao. Hallo.*"

"Tonight we shall at least have spaghetti, pepperoni, macaroni, and tutti-frutti," Oleg announced before Konstantin pushed him toward his room.

"You will get ready to perform," Konstantin replied sternly.

◇  ◇

After Voronin had checked into his room with Rustam, he sat in the window and thought of all he knew about this ancient city, an inspiration to Michelangelo and Dante, filled with the art of Leonardo. Now that he was actually here, how could he possibly stay inside and pretend he was back in the Soviet Union? He had to go out, if only for a few hours.

Rustam had fallen immediately asleep on his face, after drinking a small complimentary bottle of red wine; he was snoring loudly. Voronin had figured that since everyone would be exhausted by their journey, it would be easy to sneak out, and he was right. In fact, *sneak* wasn't even the word for it. He slipped on his coat and walked out of the room, then out a rear exit door.

It was a warm, balmy day. He jumped on the first bus that came by and got off only a few minutes later, in the middle of a busy boulevard. He walked around as Florence was just waking; deliveries were being made, people were rushing to work, cats were roaming the alleys. Merchants sprayed down their sidewalks.

He walked the streets for blocks, looking into shop windows and cafés, where Italians stood with their espresso cups and newspapers, fueling up for the day.

Voronin wandered into a café and ordered coffee and a pastry; he absorbed his surroundings with a sigh of pleasure. The city felt alive. It smelled of coffee and cologne and freshly baked bread. The sun was golden, unlike the thin white sun that shone in Moscow. He looked at his watch—he wanted to admire the gold wares on the Ponte Vecchio, to gaze at the River Arno. But there was no time for any of that. He had to return soon, or he would be in trouble.

He closed his eyes for a moment and imagined what it would be like to live as these Florentines did—with sun and freedom—without the hand of regulation and restraint always pressing down. Once again, he imagined himself in America; he felt the sun on the back of his neck. He saw himself walking up the stairs of the Magic Castle and into the ornate interior.

"My brain is the key that sets me free," he whispered, quoting his hero, Houdini, and opened his eyes.

◇　◇

The Italian performance was held in a large auditorium, which housed the huge striped tent like a shell.

The performance began with Xavier and Zoe performing their trapeze act, flying through the air like birds, to great applause. They seemed to have necks of steel when balancing on each other, and bodies of rubber. The physical grace of their performance combined with the complex display of their craft was astounding.

"Watching them still makes me nervous, even after all these years," Oleg said, peeking out through the curtain with Dmitri, both of them dressed as hobos. Suddenly Dmitri cleared his throat and gave Oleg a special nod; they had spotted Vlad and Konstantin at the front of the house.

"I'll stand guard," Oleg told Dmitri, who headed back into the dressing rooms.

He stealthily entered Mariska's dressing room, where she was working on her makeup, surrounding her eyes with a smoky kohl.

"Hello, Mariska. The show is great tonight, huh?"

Mariska eyed him suspiciously in the mirror, without stopping her preparations. "As you can see, I have not been watching. What exactly do you want, Dmitri?"

"Why do you assume I want something?"

"Why does a bird fly north for the spring?"

Dmitiri smiled. "All right, you are too smart for me. I've come because I hear that you make the most beautiful calligraphy."

"You understand wrong. I make other things beautiful, but not that."

Dmitri took out a pack of cigarettes and placed them on her vanity. "There are more where this came from."

The pack caused her to stop her preparations. She looked at the cigarettes with visible longing.

"These are very rare," she said.

"I know."

She looked back at Dmitri again and sighed.

"I don't know calligraphy myself, but I may know someone who does. See me later, when I'm done performing."

✧ ✧

Backstage, Lev stretched, getting ready for their act, while Irena sat, eating a plate of overcooked noodles and veal. Dmitri suddenly appeared at her side.

"Hello, Dmitri. How are you?"

"I'm good. And you?"

Irena sighed with obvious melancholy. "Oh, I don't know."

Dmitri set a can of chocolate sauce, a highly valued item, on the table in front of her. "Perhaps you could be better?"

Irena picked up the can of chocolate sauce and looked at him in disbelief. "For me? But why?"

"Why does there have to be a reason?" he asked in mock seriousness. "I know this is a favorite of Lev's."

"But chocolate sauce is very dear. You know this!"

"Oh, all right. Maybe I need just a little favor from you."

"It must be a big one," she said, her eyes wide.

✧ ✧

At the end of the evening's performance, Vlad urged the troupe to hurry onto the bus. They were running late.

"Let's go—we need to get back to the hotel."

The performers had collected their things and were filing out. Oleg was right behind Voronin as they departed, but he couldn't find Irena.

She was still backstage, hunched over a piece of paper—finishing up the painstaking writing of a letter, making it look as official as possible. She overheard Konstantin call out, "The bus is leaving! All aboard!"

She quickly folded the letter, placed it in a green envelope, grabbed her bag, and ran out to take her bus seat next to Mariska.

"It's like a spy movie," Mariska laughed, taking the envelope from Irena.

❖　❖

Back in the hotel, Konstantin supervised as the performers filed into their rooms.

Mariska pulled a book from her duffel bag and offered it to Dmitri.

"Here's the mystery you wanted, Dmitri. It's very scary—I hope it doesn't keep you awake all night."

"Ah, yes, thanks." Dmitri took the book and quickly turned away. Mariska smiled and lit a cigarette, inhaling luxuriously.

"Just a moment," Konstantin said suspiciously. He came over and took the book from Dmitri, then examined it, flipping through its pages, but he found nothing.

"You want to read?" Dmitri asked innocently. "Have it before me, if you want."

"No, thank you," Konstantin said coolly, giving him a dirty look as he handed back the book.

At that moment, Irena took the opportunity to slip the green envelope to Oleg.

In the middle of the hall, Konstantin yawned, then turned to Vlad, consulting his watch.

"I can take care of everything for a while," Vlad said. Konstantin nodded, then walked to the end of the hall and exited, leaving Vlad in charge.

Later that night, Dmitri and Oleg stood at their room door, listening closely.

After a moment, a door opened and closed, then they heard the Ovinko sisters talking quietly.

Oleg stuck his head out of his room, just in time to witness Vlad watching the sisters pass in their nightgowns, heading toward the bathroom. It was just as they'd hoped. The sisters, especially in nightclothes, were too alluring to resist.

Oleg tiptoed out of his room and dashed down the hall, disappearing just before Vlad turned back. Oleg approached the concierge.

"*Buona sera.*"

"*Buona sera.*" Oleg showed the concierge the letter. "Eh, could you send this letter out for me as soon as possible?"

He offered the concierge a Matryoshka nesting doll as an incentive.

"*Certamente!*" the concierge said, delighted, taking the letter and the doll. "My daughter will love this."

As soon as Oleg moved away, the concierge shook the doll and opened it to find a smaller one inside. He was thrilled.

The Ovinko sisters emerged from the bathroom, chatting among themselves as Vlad turned to watch them again.

Dmitri waved Oleg into their room, encouraging him to hurry while Vlad wasn't looking.

◇　◇

Down the hall in Irena and Lev's room, Lev reclined on the bed, frowning as he watched another cooking show, this one featuring a mustachioed Italian, who was stirring a red sauce with gusto.

"Italian cooking shows are so much better than Swiss. I don't understand one word. But they still make me hungry."

Irena was nowhere to be seen, but there was sound from the kitchenette—a can being opened.

"Don't you agree? Irena?"

Lev turned as Irena entered the room in a revealing lace negligee, with a plunging neckline and deep slits up the side. She was holding an open can of chocolate sauce on a little tray.

"Something sweet, my dear?" she said to him and held it out so that he could see.

"Chocolate sauce!" His face brightened as he saw the can; he suddenly appeared famished.

She sat down in front of him, and said, "Open, please!"

He leaned back on his pillows like a prince and closed his eyes. Irena inserted a big spoonful of sauce into his mouth, then wiped the residue from his lips.

"Ohhh, my God! It is so *good!*" Lev groaned with pleasure.

"I'm glad, my darling. You know I only want to please you."

"More, more!" he said, and Irena beamed as she gave him another spoonful.

⟡　⟡

The next afternoon, Valentine knelt in Voronin's dressing room and drove another screw into Voronin's prop table.

"There," he said, and stood up. "I added a piece of titanium as support. It should be very solid now."

Voronin tested it by placing a vase on it. It stood firm.

"Thank you, my friend. It is perfect now."

At the same moment, Oleg and Dmitri were walking near the entrance as a courier entered, carrying a green envelope. He handed it to Konstantin.

*"Ciao. Ho una lettera per Yevgeni Voronin."*

*"Grazie."*

When the courier had gone, Konstantin took out a letter opener that he kept in his coat pocket for such occasions and opened the envelope.

He read the letter, a look of increasing surprise passing over his face. The clowns watched hopefully, but all he did was fold it up and put it into his pocket. It wasn't until after the performance that Konstantin headed into Voronin's dressing room, where the magician sat, alone now, removing his makeup.

"A letter for you," Konstantin said and handed it to him with a look that betrayed some suspicion.

"For me?" Voronin excitedly took the letter from the envelope, and his eyes devoured the words.

Later, he gathered the whole troupe together in the auditorium.

As they clustered around him, he said, "Listen to this!

*"Dear Yevgeni Voronin. We have been watching you, and we are most impressed. Your demonstrated excellence in the magical arts is, without a doubt, unlike anything we have ever seen. Therefore it is with great pride and humility that the Italian chapter of the Universalist Magician's Society wishes to confer upon you the title of Honorary Grand Magician of Italy!"*

The performers applauded politely, though many looked back and forth at one another, clearly surprised. Irena averted her eyes, studying the floor as Voronin spoke. The clowns clapped more enthusiastically than anyone.

Voronin folded the letter but continued speaking with great dignity. "My friends! I can't believe it. It is so beautiful, this day. It's like a sun setting over the ocean in summer. When the waves are big, but not too big. And the air is warm, but not too warm. There's a breeze, and it's blowing, but not too hard, and this . . . letter is like a double scoop of strawberry ice cream, and it's melting, but not too fast. And you are here with me! What do I do? I don't know what to do!" He was so overcome with emotion that he stammered, but then he gathered himself. "I know! With permission from Konstantin Vasilyev, I would like to make a party for you."

Everyone cheered and looked at Konstantin, who stood on the sidelines with his inscrutable face.

"It *is* good news," Dmitri offered.

Finally Konstantin looked at his watch and said, "For one hour!"

After a moment of silence, a huge cheer erupted. A boxing bell rang. Someone began to play an accordion as the troupe pushed their way into the clown's dressing room, led by Dmitri and Oleg. The two passed around vodka bottles, which they just happened to have lined up, ready for use. The troupe exploded with pent-up celebration— playing music, dancing, singing, guzzling alcohol straight from the bottle. Oleg lay on the ground as Dmitri poured vodka straight into his mouth. A small crowd gathered around Rustam, cheering as the vodka he poured into his ear emerged from his mouth.

Still dressed in her pink wig, Svetlana walked up to Voronin and said, "Congratulations on your award."

"Thank you, thank you," Voronin said, giving a small bow. "Would you like to see it?" he added.

"Yes, of course."

He handed it to her, and she read it. Then she studied it a beat longer, turning it over and holding it up to the light.

"What's wrong?" he asked.

"Nothing. Of course, it is wonderful for you. All of us are proud." Her face looked troubled beneath her smile, but Voronin didn't notice.

Irena pulled Lev onto the dance floor, but he only danced for a moment before he pulled away from her. He then went to join the men who were involved in drinking games.

The Ovinko sisters danced with each other in a circle, holding hands, going round and round. Mariska twirled about alone, a glass in one hand, a cigarette in the other.

Konstantin watched from the sidelines with his face blank, checking his watch every few minutes. Soon another boxing bell rang, and he called out, "Party over!"

With wobbly knees, the troupe stumbled out, drunk, happy, and exhausted. Voronin, carrying a red balloon on a string, was the last to leave, a smile plastered across his face.

# CHAPTER 5

The next day, almost everyone on the bus was passed out, mouths open, arms hanging off the armrests. Dmitri and Oleg had collapsed toward each other in a snoring heap, as had Lev and Irena—she'd managed to snake her arm across his chest.

Voronin, however, was awake and beaming, practicing a new card trick with renewed confidence. Svetlana was awake, too, sitting next to him and knitting her blue hat. But by midtrip the two of them had also closed their eyes, and slept with their mouths open, slumped toward each other in their seats.

Voronin awoke with a start as they neared their next stop, Madrid, and studied Svetlana's face. Up close, her skin was like porcelain, her smell sweet as a bakery.

In the past, Voronin's dreams had always centered on his career as a magician. They were triumphal dreams. He saw himself in front of crowds of thousands, performing with perfect aplomb and breathtaking skill. When actual people entered his dream, they were ghosts of magicians from long ago, who stood in the theater aisles and applauded him or shouted out bits of advice.

But lately, during his deepest slumbers, his dreams had taken on a more romantic cast. He saw himself surrounded not just by applause, but love—there was a woman, faceless and far away, who stood in the wings, waiting for him. There were small versions of himself, a boy and girl, encircled by the woman's arms, cute and snuggly as puppies.

Where was this coming from? He'd turn 40 soon, and domestic bliss seemed a state designed for someone else. He'd been alone all his life and had never expected to have the career of his dreams and a love as well. It seemed too much to ask for. Because of this, these dreams were nearly alarming, as if he would have to give up one thing to have another.

*How have I lived alone so long?* he wondered, and at just that moment, Svetlana awoke with a start.

"Oh!" she exclaimed, blushing as she sat up and patted her hair. "I'm sorry. I didn't mean to fall asleep on you."

"No, it is fine. You keep me warm. This bus is very cold."

She gathered her sweater around her, her cheeks pink with embarrassment.

He busied himself with the road signs, then the atlas, as the bus pulled up to the hotel.

"One thousand forty-six miles, one thousand six hundred eighty-four kilometers," he announced.

"Sixteen hours! My old bones ache," Oleg complained behind them.

"You're not the only one," said Dmitri.

Voronin was ecstatic as he helped Svetlana alight from the bus. "Spain, home of the great explorers! Cortés, Ponce de León! Conquistadors. Bullfighting!"

"And don't forget the Inquisition!" Oleg added.

The clowns milled about in a nearby gift shop before entering the hotel lobby wearing matador's hats and speaking rudimentary Spanish.

At the front desk, with the Spanish flag hanging, the concierge greeted the troupe with smiles as they dragged in their luggage. "*Bienvenida. Bienvenida,*" he said.

◇   ◇

The next evening, Voronin was the last to perform. He began his act with verve and renewed confidence and made only a few mistakes. He performed his coin trick, then made a tablecloth on his table change colors.

In the wings, Valentine ran up to where Lev and Irena were watching the magician, waiting to go on.

"Voronin forgot his vase! I just found it."

Irena quickly grabbed it as Voronin looked over and realized the error. He held up his cape as Irena conspicuously walked onstage and placed it on the table. He was too late to hide her, and many in the audience laughed at this obvious blunder. Voronin continued, surprised by the quality of their laughter. It didn't sound embarrassed anymore, but deep and hearty. In fact, to his amazement, he even received guffaws when he dropped his top hat on the floor, which grew louder still when he bungled his card trick, pulling out the same card each time.

At the end of his act, the audience cheered, and he joined the troupe backstage as they gathered in high spirits.

"Encore!" Peter cried at the clapping from the audience.

The troupe ran back onstage to tremendous applause.

After a moment, they returned backstage. Konstantin was sternly waiting, looking at his watch.

Dmitri asked, "One more encore. Please?"

Konstantin shook his head. "No more. You have ten minutes to pack up."

# CHAPTER 6

That night at the hotel, Lev watched a Spanish cooking show, while Irena lay on the bed, her feet on his back, staring at the ceiling, frustration and boredom on her face.

She rolled over and looked at him.

"Lev."

"What?"

"Do you want to make love?"

His eyes were glued to the television; it was not even clear whether he'd heard her. "What's paella?" he asked.

She stormed into the bathroom and emerged a few minutes later, wearing a veil. Humming a tune, she began doing a frantic belly dance, snapping finger chimes as she circled around him.

Lev looked right through her. "I think it's something with rice; maybe fish. I'll have to look it up." He gazed at her momentarily, and her heart filled with hope, but only for a moment. "Can you stop that noise? I can't hear what he's saying."

Irena shook off her finger chimes just as there was a knock on the door. She peeked out and saw Svetlana in the hallway.

"Oh, sorry," she said, seeing Irena's costume. "I hope I'm not interrupting anything."

Irena opened the door wider so that Svetlana could see Lev glued to the television. "Unfortunately, no. Come on in."

"Can we talk—somewhere else?"

A cloud passed over Irena's face. "Sure. I'll be right out."

She threw a robe over her outfit and met Svetlana in the hallway.

"Come to my room. Mariska is out for the evening, so we're in luck."

"What do you mean, out?"

"Meeting one of her men," Svetlana said.

"She's *sneaked* out?"

"She does it all the time."

"And she never gets caught?"

"It's not so hard to manage."

They entered Svetlana's room and sat down on the edge of the bed.

"Is something wrong?" Irena asked.

"Yes, there is. I'm suspicious about Voronin's letter," she said. "I don't think it's official. I think someone else wrote it, someone in the troupe."

"Why do you think that?"

"The handwriting, it looks familiar, also feminine. And there are certain usages that are distinctly Russian."

The more Svetlana talked, the paler Irena grew. "But how did you see the letter?"

"Voronin showed me."

"Why did he do that? Are you two involved?"

Svetlana looked down with a small smile. "We are friends."

"So you really don't believe the letter is real?" Irena said.

"Not only that, but I think Mariska wrote it!"

"But why?"

"So we can have parties. It's the only good news that anyone's had." She looked at Irena's uneasy face. "Unless you've had good news with Lev, of course, and haven't mentioned it."

Irena looked abashed, then blushed. "I've tried everything. Nothing works. It's no use—he sees me as his cousin or sister."

Svetlana shook her head. "Don't give up yet. You'll see, he'll come around."

"I know you think so, but why?"

"I don't know—it's the way men are. They cannot see what is right in front of them sometimes . . . and then something happens, and their eyes open."

Irena looked at her. "Are you perhaps also talking about yourself?"

Svetlana blushed but looked away. "I give you advice as an older woman, that's all."

Irena thought for a moment. "All right, I better go now." She rose, but stopped at the door. "Let me know if you find out anything, will you?"

"Of course." Svetlana opened the door. "Good luck tonight with Lev."

"Ha!" Irena said. "With him, I need more than luck!"

&#10022;   &#10022;

As Irena returned to Lev, she passed Voronin and Rustam's room. She stopped for a minute and placed her ear at the door. She could hear Voronin chatting nonstop to a background of snores.

He was saying, "Every magician at the Magic Castle has a special team. He has a first assistant, as well as a second, backup assistant."

The snoring intensified, but Voronin's voice droned on.

"Now, if the backup assistant gets sick—hmm, what happens if the backup assistant gets sick?"

Shaking her head, Irena moved on to her own room.

&#10022;   &#10022;

Next door to Voronin, Dmitri and Oleg sat passing a bottle of vodka back and forth.

Dmitri said, "If there are no more parties, I'm going to defect. I won't be able to stand it."

"You will not defect. We will make more good news happen. Now, come on and get ready."

Dmitri wiped his mouth and eyed a red envelope on the desk by the door. "Okay, I will do it."

A few minutes later, Dmitri approached the front desk and offered the concierge a Matryoshka doll and the red envelope.

"Please? Can you arrange delivery of this letter?"

The concierge smiled. "*Sí, sí.*"

◇　◇

When a courier arrived at the circus the next day, Konstantin intercepted the envelope, opened it, and read it with a grim look.

As Voronin put on his makeup, Konstantin entered his dressing room and tossed the envelope at him.

"For me? Again?"

"Yes, all of a sudden you're very popular."

That evening, Voronin gathered everyone together again and read the new letter aloud with great drama:

"*The Spanish Chapter of the Universalist Magician's Society . . .*" He paused to explain. "This is one of the top chapters in the world, the Spanish chapter. Last year it was ranked number three, I think. Eh, where was I . . . *Spanish Chapter*—blah, blah, blah—*to present you with this diploma for your continued distinction.*"

He held up the diploma, which had arrived with the letter.

Dmitri and Oleg gave Irena a sly look of triumph.

Voronin continued, "Blah, blah, blah, *and bestow upon you our highest honor, the title of International Doctor of Magic!*"

Konstantin looked at Vladimir, then at the troupe, with clear skepticism and shrugged. "Okay, very nice."

Voronin wasn't ready to sit. "My friends! If I could take this beating heart out of my chest and chop it up small and fine, I would give a piece to each and every one of you. To thank you. For making me who I am today. But since I can't do that, please, I would like to throw a party for you! With Konstantin's permission, of course!"

Everyone cheered. Konstantin cleared his throat in warning. Then he said, begrudgingly, "Two hours."

Everyone hooted as a boxing bell was rung.

The party that night was just as exuberant as the last, yet not as frantic. The drinking was still plentiful, but the troupe took time to breathe and talk along with their dancing and singing.

Rustam and the workers brought in cases of vodka and food, while Konstantin made a note of each item of food and drink that was being consumed. Voronin walked up to him and looked at the list.

"You know you will have to pay for all of this," Konstantin remarked.

"Yes, of course. I will." He pointed at the list. "Don't forget to include crackers."

The Ovinko sisters had brought their textbooks with them to the party and read on the sidelines, even though they also sipped vodka.

Lev tangoed with Irena. When he accidentally let her spin away, Voronin was there to spin her back.

Soon most of the troupe was dancing in one large, rambunctious circle. Oleg eventually persuaded even the Ovinko sisters to put down their books and join in.

✧　✧

Mariska had left the party early, and Svetlana found her in their room, smoking with relish as she prepared to sneak out for another tryst.

Svetlana waved her hand through the gray air. "I thought we agreed that you wouldn't smoke in the room."

Mariska shrugged as she inhaled. "I was given special cigarettes as a gift, and I couldn't resist. Have one."

Svetlana shook her head. "If I have one, I will be hooked all over again. As you know."

Mariska looked at her. "You seem strange lately. Is something wrong with you?"

"Well, now that you mention it, I have been concerned about something—letters that have been written by someone in the troupe to a certain magician . . . " She opened her purse and pulled one out.

Mariska looked at it and blanched. "Well, I hope you don't think that I'm the one—"

Svetlana grimaced. "If not you, then who?"

"How would I know? Plus, this is none of your business. You go to these parties, don't you? And the letters make Voronin happy. What harm is there?"

"None. If manipulating the feelings of another human is nothing."

"He will live. He's developed quite an ego lately, I've noticed."

Svetlana felt as if steam were building in her head. "He's only been gratified by the recognition he's been receiving, for which he has worked many years," she said hotly. "Imagine what will happen when he realizes it was all a hoax."

Mariska looked at her lazily. "You seem very concerned about him. Also, how will he ever know, unless you tell him?"

Svetlana gave her a narrow look, then grabbed the knitting needles she'd come to fetch and headed back to the festivities.

✧   ✧

Toward the end of the party, Voronin found Svetlana sitting alone at a dinner table, knitting and looking unusually pensive.

"Ah, here you are. May I offer you a toast?"

Svetlana smiled. "Certainly. But for what?"

"For being yourself."

"Okay." He clinked her glass too firmly, splashing a bit of vodka.

"Sorry."

She laughed. "It's okay."

Voronin looked at her and felt something in his heart widen. "You want to see my diploma?" he asked, realizing he sounded like a boy.

Svetlana took it from him and looked at it closely.

"It's from the Spanish chapter of the—"

"Yes, I see."

"One day, I will go to the Magic Castle in Hollywood, California."

"Yes, so I hear," Svetlana said, still looking at the diploma. "How do you think they ever found you?"

"I'm not sure," he said. "Perhaps I am becoming so well known."

She handed it back to him, her face inscrutable. "Perhaps," she said.

After a moment, he asked, "Do you like magic?"

"It's okay."

"Just okay?"

She shrugged.

"What *do* you like?"

She smiled. "To laugh."

"Yes? I can be funny, too."

She looked at him tenderly. "I know you can, Voronin."

He studied her for a moment, a smile of satisfaction on his face. What was happening to him? It had been years since he had felt such warmth for a woman. And unless he was mistaken, she felt it, too.

◇　◇

Konstantin was watching them, drinking vodka, and stomping his feet, enjoying himself for the first time, as was Vlad.

Vlad said, "I think this is the best party ever! Everyone is having a good time!"

Konstantin gave him a sharp look, then nodded twice—first with agreement, then with warning.

◇   ◇

On the bus from the hotel to the big top the next morning, Vlad and Konstantin wore dark sunglasses to shield their eyes from the harsh sun. They sat with their mouths unhinged and their arms hanging like everyone else, moaning about their aching heads and queasy stomachs.

Voronin, wearing a blue knit cap, and Svetlana, working on another piece, were the only ones happy to be awake and on the road again. They sat side by side, their shoulders touching, both of their faces aglow.

Voronin turned to her. "You really think I'm funny?"

"Yes."

"Do you want me to be funny now?"

"No. You don't have to be anything with me. Just who you are."

He turned and smiled at his reflection in the window, adjusting his new hat.

*Is this what love is like?* he wondered, looking at himself. He felt slightly seasick, but they were on dry land; he was somewhat giddy, though there was nothing funny happening. His vision seemed clearer, as if he were wearing glasses, and his hearing was suddenly more acute. It was the oddest combination—part of him felt ill, and the other part felt sharper than he'd ever been in his life.

*Maybe I am ill, after all,* he thought as he closed his eyes.

⋄  ⋄

That evening, before a rapt crowd, Voronin performed his act with flair and a new light-hearted style. When he did his coin trick, he let the coins cascade out of his fist and fall onto the floor. When he pulled out a bouquet of flowers to set them in the vase, he ended up holding up only a bouquet of stems with the flowers missing. The audience laughed. He used the situation to his advantage and wiggled his fingers at the bouquet as if making the flowers bloom. The audience laughed even harder.

Sensing that the crowd was on his side, Voronin wiggled his fingers at the audience and threw a handful of glittery confetti. They cheered.

Svetlana stood in the wings, watching and giggling. "Isn't he wonderful?" she asked Dmitri, who looked at Oleg and raised his eyebrows.

# CHAPTER 7

Paris was the next stop—a journey of more than 1,200 kilometers. Voronin was so ecstatic that he remained awake every hour of the trip. Next to America, this was the place he'd dreamed of most.

He sat talking Svetlana's ear off about Paris in literature, on stage, and in film: Balzac, Zola, *Les Misérables, Phantom of the Opera.* When she fell asleep, he talked to whomever was awake.

He got off the bus first, with Svetlana behind him, and exclaimed, "Paris, the city of light and *crêpes Suzette!*"

"And don't forget the cancan and Toulouse-Lautrec!" Svetlana added.

"No time for that!" Konstantin intoned. "Take an hour, and that's it."

❖　❖

All of the troupe, except for Dmitri and Oleg, headed to a restaurant next door for lunch, convinced by Irena that they should at least have one fine Parisian meal.

Svetlana sat beside Voronin, and he draped his arm over her shoulder as they shared a menu.

"I don't know what anything is, but I think we should pick one of everything," Svetlana said.

"Yes, this is the best idea!" Voronin agreed. "And all of it's on me."

They started with red wine and proceeded to a dizzying array of unknown dishes—all delicious—that they passed around. One was a crock of beans baked with sausage and ham; another was pizza with an egg on top; another was a baked concoction of ham, croissant, and béchamel sauce. They had raw oysters and onion soup and escargots, buttery with garlic sauce, which Svetlana and Voronin ate by themselves, feeding each other with a tiny silver fork. Voronin was reeling from the wine and the delicious food and the heady sensation of being so close to Svetlana. His heart felt as if it had swollen to twice its size and now inhabited the entirety of his chest.

Instead of having a meal, Dmitri and Oleg headed out together to the nearest park.

Oleg asked, "Okay, what's your big idea this time? We can't do another letter already."

Dmitri said, "I have an idea. Just follow me."

In the park, they found a large birch tree with low-hanging branches. "Boost me up," Dmitri said and broke off a dangling branch, then teetered and came tumbling down.

By the time they checked into the hotel, Oleg had the branch under his arm. Dmitri had acquired a beret, Sergey was playing Parisian music on his accordion, and Voronin and Svetlana were sharing a chocolate croissant, licking their fingers. At the front desk, with the French flag hanging on the wall, the concierge greeted them. "*Bienvenue. Bienvenue,*" he said.

⋄ ⋄

At the hotel, Svetlana intercepted Irena in the hallway as they headed toward their rooms.

She took her aside and whispered, "Take a nap and get rested. You and I are going out tonight—"

"Out! What do you mean? It's forbidden."

"Mariska has sneaked out on every trip, and she hasn't been caught—not once," Svetlana said. "I'm not leaving Paris without seeing the Moulin Rouge. We'll wait till Konstantin goes to sleep. Come with me!"

"Oh, I couldn't. Lev—"

"We won't tell Lev until later; he can go drinking with the boys, if he wants. This is your problem with him, Irena—you're too easy. You are always there, begging for him with your puppy eyes. Tonight he will see how it feels when you're not at his disposal."

"But Svet—"

"Don't you trust me?"

This question hit a nerve in Irena, who lowered her eyes, then nodded gravely. "Of course I do."

"Then meet me in the lobby at nine o'clock. I know what I'm doing."

❖ ❖

"So who is it tonight?" Svetlana asked Mariska, who was sitting in front of the mirror, applying extra mascara.

"He's a count, if you really must know."

"A count!" Svetlana laughed out loud. "Ha! I'll bet."

"Your sarcasm is not attractive," Mariska said, looking at her coldly in the mirror. "You will be an old maid acting so ironic and sitting alone here night after night with your knitting."

"Well, we'll see about that," Svetlana replied.

Mariska watched Svetlana brush her hair, slip on a pair of earrings, and rummage in her suitcase for high heels.

"There they are," she said to herself. They were dusty black pumps, far out of style, but she put them on anyway.

"So maybe you're doing a bit of sneaking around yourself," Mariska said.

"I'll never tell," Svetlana said with a wink, as she grabbed her purse and left.

❖ ❖

Svetlana and Irena emerged from the hotel and jumped quickly into a taxi. Irena was excited but nervous; she looked up at their window to see if the light was on, but Svetlana chastised her. "Forget Lev for a few hours—we may never be in Paris again!"

She leaned forward and told the cab driver, "The Moulin Rouge."

The driver looked back at them in the rearview mirror. "You ladies are Russian?"

"Yes! It's our first night—I guess you can tell."

"If you forgive me for being so blunt, the Moulin Rouge is a tourist trap. Not what I'd recommend for two women like you. It is not what it used to be."

Svetlana blushed. "We want a place where we can dance a little and have a good time. This is the only name I know."

"I have a place for this—and it is still in Montmartre, the same district. Would you like me to give you a little tour along the way?" he asked.

"Oh, please!" Irena said, getting into the spirit.

He did a U-turn and cut through the heart of Paris—the two women pressing their faces to the opposite windows of the cab as they took in the sights.

The cab driver intoned the highlights as they passed them.

"The Tuileries, the Champs d'Elysees, the Arc de Triomphe, the Louvre."

Irena and Svetlana looked at each other, beaming. Later he said, "And here is Les Deux Magots, a very famous café where all the writers and intellectuals met. Maybe you would like to go in and see?"

"Have you been there?" Irena asked.

"Oh, yes, of course."

Svetlana's face was aglow. "What did you have?"

He shrugged. "I don't remember; something simple. Maybe onion soup and a glass of wine."

Svetlana looked at Irena and then back at the cab driver. "Would you come back for us in an hour if we went in and ordered just a little bite? Neither one of us had dinner."

"I'll do better than that—I'll come in with you," he said. He screeched to a halt and parked.

"Come, I will get us a good table."

The two women linked arms and followed him in, both of them aglow.

After they ate, the cab driver dropped them off at a dance club that featured a glowing disco ball and blasting French music. "You will find a little bit of every kind of music here," the driver said, walking with them to the door.

The dance floor was packed with people of all ages. Once they got a table and ordered champagne, Svetlana and Irena headed onto the floor together. But they didn't dance together for long.

"*Pardon, mademoiselles,*" an accented voice interrupted. "My friend and I do not like to see two such beauties dancing together. May we?"

The women eyed the men, both middle-aged Frenchmen wearing expensive suits and shiny patent-leather shoes. The older one wore glasses and sported a mustache, while the other had dazzling white teeth and an open-collared shirt.

"Yes, why not?" Svetlana said, and she whirled off in one direction with the older of the two, leaving Irena in the arms of the other.

These were the first, but not the last, men to approach them. By the time they decided to leave, it was almost midnight, and Svetlana's feet were so swollen that she had to walk barefoot to the door.

"Can you believe it? I've never seen so many men in my life."

"I know!" Irena laughed. "I don't know what most of them said, but the dancing was so fun!"

"Ah, we deserve it," Svetlana said, as she hailed a cab back to the hotel. "It's good to see what's out in the world, eh?"

✧   ✧

The next morning over breakfast, Svetlana and Irena sat together in a corner, giggling. Voronin entered the room and came up to them. "Good morning, ladies. What is so funny?"

Svetlana whispered. "Don't tell Konstantin, but two good friends had a wild and happy time last night at a Paris club, dancing and drinking champagne."

"Svetlana!" Lev walked in with a stormy face. "Where did you take her last night? Why is she acting like this—so giddy and strange?"

Svetlana said coolly, "I don't know. You'll have to ask her."

"I have; she said she went out with you, but that's all. She didn't get back until one in the morning, and she had champagne on her breath."

"Not only that, but she was the belle of the ball—many men wanted to dance with her!"

Irena blushed. "You, too, Svetlana!"

Lev's face turned crimson. "Irena, you didn't—"

"What?" she asked haughtily. "I did dance, and very well, as Svetlana said. I had many courtly partners."

"But it's forbidden—plus you're my—"

"Your what? Steady? Fiancée? After ten years, Lev, I don't know what I am. We are not married, and until we are, what I do is my business, if you want to be strict about it."

Lev looked astonished as the two women smiled at each other over the rims of their cups.

Voronin's expression was more complex than Lev's. His face flashed with amusement, then admiration, then something else that Svetlana registered, looking up at him, even if she could not name exactly what it was.

◇   ◇

That morning, in a back room of the circus, Oleg swept up wood shavings as Dmitri stood guard. Sergey blew off the final shavings from a wand he'd carved from the branch. He handed it to Rustam, who was ready with a brush and a can of gold paint.

Rustam said, "Are you sure this is going to work?"

Oleg said, "Sure, why not? Just paint it—pronto."

Dmitri sneaked past Vlad, who was watching the Ovinko sisters rehearse, grabbed a chair, and reached up to remove a crystal from the chandelier.

Meanwhile, Voronin was in his dressing room, working with Valentine on his prop table again. "Now I want you to take the screws and titanium out."

Valentine was confused. "But I don't get it. It will fall down. It will be less solid. You want that?"

"Yes, yes. You'll see. It will be funny."

Konstantin entered the dressing room.

"Pardon me, Yevgeni Voronin."

"Yes?"

"This is for you."

Voronin was surprised that Konstantin was addressing him deferentially as he held out the parcel.

Konstantin hesitated before he left. "I ordered extra bottles of vodka. Just in case."

"Thank you."

Konstantin nodded, shaking his head as he left.

⋄  ⋄

That evening Voronin stood in front of the gathered troupe feeling more pride than ever. He looked out over the faces and thought of how long he'd known these people, many of them since they'd been very young. Why, Lev had been a mere boy of 13 or so and Irena not much older when he first worked with them. They were his family now, his confidantes. It had taken him a while to find his correct place among them, but now that he had, he cherished it.

"My friends. As you can see, I have received another great honor: *la Baguette d'Or.* The Golden Wand of France."

He showed them the wand that Rustam had carved, with a chandelier crystal at its tip, along with a new note. The wand was obviously home-made, but no one said a word about that.

Voronin continued, "I wish I could express my feelings with words, but I can't get my mouth to make the sounds. You see, because my soul is overflowing with gratitude, and my mouth, I think, is worried about my soul, and so my lips, they just keep flap-flap-flapping, and the feeling, where is it, who can say? At the Magic Castle, they have a saying—"

The boxing bell rang before he even finished, and another party broke out, this one with French accordion music filling the air. There was more dancing than ever. Voronin and Svetlana swept around the room, moving with grace and ease, as if they'd been dancing together all their lives. Sergey tap-danced. There was a wild feeling of abandonment and joy. The Ovinkos had kicked off their shoes and were doing an improvised cancan that showed off their shapely legs.

Voronin said to Svetlana, "Look at Konstantin! He's really joined the celebrations."

Rustam, Vlad, Dmitri, and Oleg paraded a drunken and whooping Konstantin around, lifting him up on a chair, much to the delight of the troupe. But it was Lev and Irena who were the real surprise; Lev kept his arm around Irena's back and held her close as they danced. As Voronin waltzed by with Svetlana, Irena smiled at her and mouthed, "Thank you."

Then Lev caught Svetlana's eye. "Big news," he announced. "We're getting married as soon as I can get the papers."

Svetlana eyed her friend, who gave her a meaningful look.

"Well, congratulations—to you both."

"Yes, it's about time, don't you think?" Lev asked, and spun Irena around and headed in the other direction.

A conga line had formed near the exit. The whole troupe joined in just as the boxing bell rang, conga-dancing into the concierge's area and down the hotel hall.

# CHAPTER 8

The next morning on the bus, the troupe snored while Voronin and Svetlana were alert. He was still wearing his new cap, and his face was lit with pleasure. Svetlana rested her head on his shoulder and her hand over his. Far in the back of the bus, Irena wrote one last letter by hand.

The troupe arrived late at a Portuguese hotel near Lisbon. They brought in no souvenirs this time and dragged their luggage behind them with a mixed look of exhaustion and nausea. The concierge greeted them with *"Bem-vindos,"* but they barely responded.

The next day, Svetlana worked with Voronin, helping him sew together a shirt with a quick-release collar. When she was done, he practiced reaching into his hat for the red rope.

"Yes, yes, that is good," she said, encouragingly.

"Do you really think so?"

"Yes, especially if you stand like so . . ." She positioned herself to show him.

"We are a team now, maybe?" Voronin said.

She smiled. "Yes, maybe we are."

◇   ◇

Later that evening, Oleg sneaked out of his hotel room, a brown envelope in hand.

Soon after, Voronin stood backstage before the troupe.

"And now, my friends, may I introduce you to a dear friend of mine from back home."

Peter rolled out a table with a large bowl.

"Caviar!"

A large cake was also rolled out, covered with buttercream icing.

The party immediately commenced.

"Have you ever heard of so many honors?" a workman muttered.

"Have you ever seen so many celebrations?" another said.

Konstantin guzzled vodka, laughing with Sergey and Peter. There was wild, shirtless dancing by the men and much laughter.

It was past midnight when the troupe ate dinner together as one big, tipsy family; there were fresh lobsters and shrimp and champagne and sweet pastries. It would be their last supper on the road, all of them together, but they didn't realize it yet.

◇   ◇

In the wings the next evening, the troupe gathered at the curtain to watch Voronin. There was something special about his performance tonight. The audience was laughing louder than ever, and there was uproarious applause.

Onstage, Voronin was about to set his flowers in the vase when the table fell over—just as he'd intended. He shrugged and looked cross-eyed; the audience laughed raucously, as did the troupe.

Dmitri moved closer to Oleg and said, "I don't know what he's doing, but he's hilarious."

Voronin pulled the red rope out of his magic hat. The rope retracted rapidly, and he grabbed for it in vain. His shirt got caught on something inside the hat, and his entire shirt was pulled off into the hat. The audience roared. With false modesty, Voronin covered his chest. Then he held a curtain up over his front and was dressed again by the time he let it down.

Svetlana and the troupe cheered. Voronin felt transformed by the wave of laughter emerging from the audience. He looked out at them, absorbing it. This was what he had yearned for all his life—this adoration and affection. He felt the laughter as if tendrils of energy were floating from the audience and directly entering his body. He felt more alive than ever.

He turned to Svetlana, who gave him a warm smile that pierced his heart. She was a large part of this new feeling—she was the one who had helped him believe in what was innate in him, who had encouraged him to tap into his deepest talent.

With that, the rest of his act became effortless, one uproarious move after another, as he simply became his real self and embraced being funny. He dropped coins and pulled wrong cards from the deck. He used these mistakes for humor, and the crowd clapped and cheered heartily.

When he finished and returned backstage, there was a roar of approval and backslapping. Looking at his friends and at Svetlana's blushing face, he felt utterly happy. This time when there was a refrain for an encore, Konstantin joined in, clapping and telling them all to take another bow.

◇   ◇

After the show, the troupe gathered around Konstantin, who told them he had an important announcement for them all.

"Today I received word that we will not be traveling on to Greece," he told them.

There was a look of confusion among the troupe members.

"So where will we be going?" Voronin asked

Konstantin said, "Home. Tomorrow we go home. The bus will leave at eight o'clock, so don't be late."

"But why?" Dmitri asked.

"Because the tour is over," Konstantin answered. He would say no more.

Silence and sad looks. No one knew quite what to do. Some of the troupe began heading for the door.

Konstantin added, "Wait. There is something more. I have a letter here from Hollywood, California, Voronin. I believe it's for you."

Dumbstruck, Voronin walked up to claim the letter. He hadn't expected anything further after the Golden Wand. He read the letter to himself, then read it again. He felt tears rise in his eyes and a lump gather in his throat. He was afraid to speak until he looked at Svetlana, who nodded at him, as if to say, "It's okay."

"It's from the Magic Castle," he said softly.

Irena and Mariska looked at Dmitri and Oleg, who pretended to know nothing about it.

"And . . . ?"

"It's from the Magic Castle!"

"Yes, Voronin, we understand that, but is there anything else you would like to say?"

Voronin was on the verge of tears.

"Just that I am the luckiest man in the world."

# CHAPTER 9

Back in Moscow, the troupe stood before the minister of culture, who moved down the line and offered each one of them his hand.

"Thank you for your work, thank you."

After congratulating each of them individually, he addressed the group as a whole.

"Excellent job. All of you. You have brought honor to your country. As a reward, you have each been granted a four-month sabbatical."

There were excited looks among the troupe members.

"Unpaid, of course."

Excited looks turned to disappointment.

"During this time, you will have ample opportunity to rest, to nurse your injuries, and to visit with family and friends. I trust that each of you has made enough to make do until then, assuming you have saved wisely. Welcome home."

The troupe began filing out of the office with despondent faces.

"Minister, may I have two minutes of your time, sir?" Voronin asked.

The minister looked surprised by the brazen request, but he also appeared intrigued. He turned to the others. "Will you excuse us, please?"

As they left, Oleg, Dmitri, and Svetlana looked back in trepidation to see Voronin pulling the envelopes out of his bag to show the minister.

Konstantin closed the door on them, shutting the troupe out and Voronin in.

"He's a dead man," Oleg murmured to Dmitri.

Dmitri frowned. "So are we."

In the minister's office, Voronin laid out the letters, the diploma, and the wand on the desk before him. There were more letters and other trinkets that he hadn't shown to anyone else, even Svetlana. Before this trip, he would have felt nervous approaching the minister so personally, but now he possessed a new core of self-confidence.

He said to the minister, "Please, look at this. Italy, Switzerland, Spain. All of them celebrating my work as an artist."

The minister picked up the letters and studied them, then the wand.

"It is the Golden Wand of France, la Baguette d'Or."

❖　❖

Dmitri and Oleg were sitting on the bench outside the minister's office, anxiously tapping their feet, waiting for Voronin to emerge.

"Siberia, that's where they'll send us," Dmitri said.

"I hope," said Oleg.

"You hope?"

"It could be worse."

⋄  ⋄

Svetlana was sitting at the end of another bench, having a talk with Irena, who had caught up with her as she was walking out.

"Our Paris outing did the trick. Lev was so jealous that he won't let me out of his sight. He has told me he loves me three times since. And tonight he has a big surprise, he says!"

Svetlana gave her a hug. "I knew he'd see the light, Irena. I am so glad."

When they drew apart, Irena's face had grown solemn. "That is the good thing I wanted to tell you. But, Svetlana, I have to tell you something else not so good. I was the one who—"

Svetlana held up her hand. "Don't say more."

"But you're my friend. And so is Voronin. I feel so guilty."

"Please," Svetlana said. "After our talk, I realized that you were probably the one. But I decided that the letters did no harm. They actually helped Voronin. They made him believe in himself."

"You knew all along? Why did you not tell him?"

"I didn't want to spoil it for him. He would have been devastated to find out the letters weren't true. There is a quotation by Houdini that Voronin loves: 'What the eyes see and the ears hear, the mind believes.'"

✧   ✧

Inside the office, Voronin wrapped up his meeting with the minister by pulling out the letter from the Magic Castle.

"And finally, most important of all, this is from the Magic Castle in Hollywood, California, the most wonderful place in all the world."

The minister read the letter.

"You see, minister, this is why I can't go on holiday," Voronin said. "Not because of money—take everything from me, I will perform anywhere—but because of magic. You see? For example, this is a very good position, but one day you will retire from the ministry. And that's great! But me, I will never retire. Never. This is not just a job for me. I am a magician. I can make the impossible possible. I can make the ordinary extraordinary. With magic, I can make people laugh. With real magic, you can open people's hearts."

The minister considered his words. "Do you know what I could do to you for having contact with the West?"

Voronin remained silent.

"Do you?"

Voronin said, "Yes, minister. Of course I do."

◇  ◇

In the lobby, Oleg looked at his watch.

"What's taking so long?

"Maybe they'll let him off with a warning," Dmitri said.

"And then what?" Oleg asked. "He goes home penniless."

Svetlana put her head in her hands.

A sudden exclamation of joy came from the minister's office. The door flew open and Voronin stepped out, arms open wide. "The minister is going to throw a party for me!"

Dmitri and Oleg looked at each other in disbelief. Svetlana jumped to her feet and rushed into Voronin's arms.

# CHAPTER 10

The auditorium at the Ministry of Culture was decorated with red crepe; a punch bowl stood in the back, overseen by a florid middle-aged woman who discreetly spiked it with a bottle of vodka when no one was watching.

Not only were the troupe members in the audience, but also the neighborhood locals who had sat in on performances in the past in order to get out of the cold.

Voronin sat on a raised dais in his best black suit, among various officials wearing banners and military regalia.

The cultural minister stood gravely and approached Voronin with a large medal on a chain. He put it around Voronin's neck and then spoke to the assembled crowd. "Along with this medal of achievement and appreciation, Voronin, you have been provided with your own traveling circus. Congratulations!"

A cheer rose up as the troupe jumped to their feet and applauded. Cameras flashed and popped.

Voronin bowed, posed, and waved, then descended the platform to walk arm in arm with Svetlana through the small throng of well-wishers.

Dmitri called out, "Hey, Voronin, maybe you need some good clowns for your new show, eh?"

"Call me!" Voronin said as he and Svetlana kept walking.

Svetlana gave a wink as they walked by Irena and Lev; Irena hugged Svetlana and held up her hand, which was sporting an engagement ring.

When Voronin turned and saw what Svetlana was looking at, he led her into the hallway and into a secluded doorway. Then he took both her hands in his and faced her. "I might not need good clowns, but there is someone I do need. Do you know who?"

Svetlana lowered her gaze and blushed. "I think so."

"I think I have fallen in love with you, Svetlana. Will you join me in my dreams?"

She looked up into his face with great feeling. "I already have, Voronin."

He drew her to him, and they gave each other a long and passionate kiss, as the rest of the troupe peeked around the corner, beaming with delight.

# EPILOGUE

"Max, come on!" My sister broke into my reverie as she walked down the hallway from the other direction. How long had I been standing here, looking at the photos of the world's greatest magicians and illusionists? It felt like only moments, but from her face, I saw that it must have been a long while.

"Papa's ready to go on. We have to take our seats!"

All at once, I heard a wave of laughter and applause. According to my mother, there were three performance spaces here at the Magic Castle: the Parlor of Prestidigitation, which re-created an old-fashioned parlor experience; the Close-up Gallery, which housed masters of close-up magic; and the Palace of Mystery. That was where we were headed.

A longtime friend of our family, an old man named Oleg, came out and removed a sign that read *Jorge the Illusionist* and replaced it with another that said in even larger letters, *Direct from the Four Corners of the Earth: Voronin the Magnificent— Magician Extraordinaire!*

"Svetlana, bring the kids and hurry," Oleg called.

"Max!" my mother called.

"Just a minute!" Through the window, I saw two people arriving who were just as excited as I was about tonight's performance.

Luckily the door was partly ajar, so I pushed it open all the way, and there was a gaunt man leaning heavily on two canes, accompanied by his elderly mother. He was dressed in a bow tie and a shiny suit jacket that had seen better days. His thin hair was slicked back, his face aglow. The elderly woman had on a fur hat despite the warm weather, and was wearing a rhinestone necklace.

"You made it!" I exclaimed.

"We would not miss it," Mrs. Komarov said. "Would we, Ivan?"

"No, never." Ivan smiled. "Even if we had to pay for tickets ourselves!"

"Hey, Max! Come on!" my sister called out.

"Your papa is going on," my mother added, waving me toward her.

She didn't have to call again—after a quick wave to my friends, I ran to her, anxious to get in: I was going to experience the most exciting event possible in my life. I was going to watch my father fulfill his fondest dream—performing at the Magic Castle as one of the world's greatest magicians.

# ABOUT THE AUTHORS

**Sophia Max** lives in Austin, Texas, and writes books about rock climbing, the martial arts, and the spiritual unknown.

**Lynn Lauber** is a fiction and nonfiction author, teacher, and book collaborator. She has published three books of her own with W. W. Norton & Co., as well as many collaborations with other authors. Her specialties include fiction, personal narrative, and self-improvement. Her essays have appeared in *The New York Times.* She has abridged audio books for such authors as John Updike, Oliver Sacks, Oprah Winfrey, and Gore Vidal.
Website: **www.lynnlauber.com**

# Also Available

## *Painting the Future*
### DVD with Bonus Material • $14.95

Inspired by the writings of best-selling author Louise L. Hay, *Painting the Future* reveals how the thoughts we choose create the life we live.

On the second floor of a low-income apartment complex lives Jonathan Page. Once an established painter, Page now lives in complete darkness, rarely leaving his apartment and angry at the world. From the courtyard below, nine-year-old Lupe Saldana takes notice of Jonathan. Determined to save up for a dream quinceañera dress, Lupe extends herself as hired help for all the personal errands and daily chores that Jonathan can no longer do himself. Through this proposition, a friendship begins to blossom, and Lupe's optimistic innocence slowly breaks down the wall of Jonathan's guarded brokenness.

## *My Greatest Teacher*
### DVD with Bonus Material • $14.95

Based on the true life story of best-selling author Dr. Wayne W. Dyer, *My Greatest Teacher* is a compelling drama that explores the transformational power of forgiveness.

Dr. Ryan Kilgore is a college professor struggling to take his career to his desired level of success, while battling the very demons that are keeping him from achieving it. Kilgore is tormented by the memories of his father's abandonment, yet his wife and child are the ones who pay the price. Upon losing his grandmother, Kilgore desperately seeks the closure that he needed so long ago as he puts his future in jeopardy for a journey into the past. Through a series of mysterious and serendipitous events, a path opens that leads Kilgore to his father—and to making the choice to rebuild everything he has destroyed as a result of what had been destroying him.

## Entanglement
DVD with Bonus Material • $14.95

Based on the writings of best-selling author and visionary scientist Gregg Braden, *Entanglement* explores the possibility of quantum entanglement and our connection to "the Divine Matrix."

When a daunting premonition takes U.S. art student Jack Franklin hostage, he is consumed by the thought of the danger his twin brother, Charlie, may be in. Separated by the war in Afghanistan and the constraints of modern-day technology, Jack defies the laws of science when he taps into the unexplainable physics of the Divine Matrix to try to save the life of his brother, as well as the lives of others serving with him.

Order Your Copies Today!
DVDs Available Exclusively at
**www.hayhouse.com**

**VISIONS**

Hay House, Inc., P.O. Box 5100, Carlsbad, CA 92018-5100
(760) 431-7695 or (800) 654-5126
(760) 431-6948 (fax) or (800) 650-5115 (fax)
**www.hayhouse.com®** • **www.hayfoundation.org**

We hope you enjoyed this Hay House book. Sign up for our
exclusive free e-newsletter featuring special offers, contests,
behind-the-scenes author interviews, movie trailers, and even
more bonus content, with the latest information on exciting
new Hay House products.

Sign Up Here

**Also Visit www.HealYourLife.com**

The destination website for inspiration, affirmations, wisdom,
success, and abundance. Find exclusive book reviews,
captivating video clips, live streaming radio, and much more!

www.hayhouse.com®      www.healyourlife.com®      www.hayhouseradio.com®

**25th ⊕HAY HOUSE Anniversary**

*Published and distributed in Australia by:*
Hay House Australia Pty. Ltd., 18/36 Ralph St.,
Alexandria NSW 2015 • *Phone:* 612-9669-4299
*Fax:* 612-9669-4144 • www.hayhouse.com.au

*Published and distributed in the United Kingdom by:*
Hay House UK, Ltd., 292B Kensal Rd., London W10 5BE
*Phone:* 44-20-8962-1230 • *Fax:* 44-20-8962-1239
www.hayhouse.co.uk

*Published and distributed in the Republic of South Africa*
*by:* Hay House SA (Pty), Ltd., P.O. Box 990, Witkoppen 2068
*Phone/Fax:* 27-11-467-8904 • www.hayhouse.co.za

*Published in India by:* Hay House Publishers India,
Muskaan Complex, Plot No. 3, B-2, Vasant Kunj,
New Delhi 110 070 • *Phone:* 91-11-4176-1620
*Fax:* 91-11-4176-1630 • www.hayhouse.co.in

*Distributed in Canada by:* Raincoast,
9050 Shaughnessy St., Vancouver, B.C. V6P 6E5
*Phone:* (604) 323-7100 • *Fax:* (604) 323-2600
www.raincoast.com

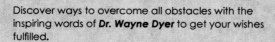

CPSIA information can be obtained at www.ICGtesting.com
Printed in the USA
LVOW061548240512

283130LV00002B/1/P